Dale the Uniclyde
An Adventure in Friendship

By Byron von Rosenberg
Illustrated by Heather Parrott

A horse with a single horn
Set between its eyes!
A pair of wings so powerful
That majestically it flies!
Except for little Dale,
Born of Clydesdale breed,
Who got a pair of tiny wings
Much smaller than he'd need.
A Clydesdale with a horn and wings?
He truly was unique
But since he couldn't fly
He got called a freak.

They picked a special name for him
And he was classified
As the one and only
Dale the Uniclyde.

Dale went about his work as other horses do
And every bit, except his wings, got stronger as he grew.
He learned to lay them flat and flicked his mane just right
So everyone forgot, but he'd shake them out at night.

He'd practice for an hour, sometimes three or four,
But his wings were just the same as they had been before.
His horse sense said he'd never fly no matter how he tried
But there was a magic growing in Dale the Uniclyde.

The other horses saw it
In his attitude
As did the stableboy
Who brought him extra food.

At night
he'd come to groom him
and stroke those tiny wings.
Attention, care, and love —
These are magic things!

For one night as he stroked Dale's back
the boy jumped and hollered out
For with his kindly touch Dale's wings began to sprout!
By morning they were ten feet long, much too big to hide,
And no one laughed that day at Dale the Uniclyde.

He ran out in the paddock and shook his mane and tail,
Then spread his mighty wings just like a giant sail.
He felt the wind beneath him and then the earth was gone
As Dale the Uniclyde soared into the dawn.

The stableboy watched proudly as tears rolled down his cheeks
For a friend finds joy when a friend finds the dream he seeks.
It took him many years but when he finally hit his stride
There was never such a horse . . .

as Dale the Uniclyde!

And the stableboy, whose name was Jim,
Changed that day as well
For a good turn alters life
In ways we cannot tell.
Jim walked and talked with confidence
And his eyes were filled with joy
And his manner said to everyone,
"I'm no longer just a boy.
I'm a man who has a vision
Of what my life can be
Because I helped a friend
And gave my all for free.
The magic in his wings
Comes from deep inside
And I'm better for the time I spent
With Dale the Uniclyde."

LIKE DALE,
THE UNICLYDE!

AUTHOR'S NOTES

I am surprised at how much of my life has been spent going about my regular duties and obligations and how much I have missed in my fifty years on the planet. And yet I have been so incredibly fortunate to write a few stories that simply opened themselves to me. **Dale the Uniclyde** is one of those ...

In May of 2006 I was given the wonderful opportunity to sign books at Grant's Farm here in the St. Louis area. They have llamas and I am the author of a little book called **I Don't Want to Kiss a Llama!** (The title was given to me by my daughter Erin.) Besides the llamas they have a tram ride through the park, wonderful animal shows, and an extraordinarily friendly and helpful staff. A highlight of the day is the chance to visit the Clydesdales!

One guest saw my name tag and, thinking I was a staff member, asked me where the Clydesdales were. I explained and then handed him a copy of my poem "Leading the Unicorn" and told him to "take my horse with you!" In that instant it came to me to write a poem about a unicorn Clydesdale. The next day I composed the poem in our car as Sharon drove us to Branson for another signing.

I have looked at my original version in my notebook several times and am amazed at how few changes I made in the story as I wrote it. The pictures were another story ...

I never planned to illustrate my own books, but I wanted **I Don't Want to Kiss a Llama!** to be affordable for families so I did it myself. It has had a very good reception from my readers and many in the graphic art field, but as I drew Dale I hesitated because of the different nature of the poem. And then, my son Ryan introduced Sharon and me to Heather Parrott who drew the alicorn (winged unicorn) on the opposite page. It wasn't long afterwards that we asked her to draw all the pictures! And aren't they wonderful?

I feel personally very close to this poem and this book because my father's name was Dale, and it was a prayer and a poem for him in 2002 that began my writing career. And so it is with the very best of wishes for you and the ones you love that I thank you for the opportunity to share this story. May the best of your dreams always come true!

Sincerely,

Byron von Rosenberg
Byrnes Mill, Missouri

Other Books by Byron von Rosenberg:

Don't Feed the Seagulls (2003) 0-975-985-833 **Climb the Red Mountain** (2004) 0-975-985-841
I Don't Want to Kiss a Llama! (2004) 0-975-985-809 **Thinking Upside Down** (2005) 0-975-985-825
O Christmas Treed! (2006) 0-975-985-85X

And keep on the lookout for:

Stars to Chase
Diamonds of the Dawn

Dale the Uniclyde
Copyright © 2007 Byron von Rosenberg and Heather Parrott
All rights reserved.

Packaged by Pine Hill Graphics

Publisher's Cataloging-in Publication-Data
(Provided by Cassidy Cataloguing Services, Inc.)

Von Rosenberg, Byron.

Dale the uniclyde : an adventure in friendship / by Byron von
Rosenberg ; illustrated by Heather Parrott. -- 1st ed. -- Byrnes Mill,
MO : Red Mountain Creations, 2007.

p. ; cm.
ISBN: 978-0-9759858-6-1

1. Friendship--Juvenile poetry. 2. Animals, Mythical—Juvenile
poetry. 3. Clydesdale horse—Juvenile poetry. 4. [Imaginary
creatures] 5. [Stories in rhyme] I. Parrott, Heather.

PZ7.V933 D35 2007
[E]--dc22   0710

Printed in China.